1

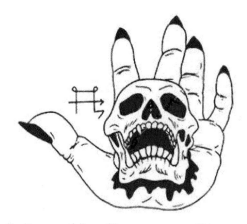

War Between Covens

Index

Synopsis- Characters

This is the story of rivalries between two Covens. Friends, which extends to their Covens (occult groups).

On the side of New Orleans is Cedric, caucasian, leader of the Coven "Hidden Hand". Cedric had short brown hair and a talisman on his chest, tattooed neck. He was an experienced hougan in voodoo and knew how to do witchcraft from different magical systems.

His girlfriend is Emma. Pretty, white, and with long hair. She loves to drink gin. She is a proficient witch and fortune-teller, occasionally possesses the ability to channel spirits, and possesses the ability to perform incorporation mediumship.

Leonard is a friend and member of the coven. A red-haired man with spiky hair wears a shirt all the time. He has extensive experience in Santeria. Coven "Hidden Hand" is not limited to a magical system; they practice different systems depending on the group's objectives.

Evelyn is a transgender individual who has undergone a gender transition surgery, resulting in her transition to a woman. She has dreadlocks. She's psychic, does remote viewing, and even has the gift of healing with her hands.

Coven also has other secondary characters such as Penelope, Zoey, Wilbur, and John.

Penelope is a lesbian who wears glasses and has short, dark hair. She usually wears a black leather coat. She has a crush on Evelyn. She is a Wicca witch.

The Coven "Nightshadow Dew" is located in the city of Baton Rouge, in the state of Louisiana, further south.

Jonas was once a close friend and now a rival. He is white and has short, punk spiky hair. He also has a beard and mustache. He often wears metal chains and amulets.

Isabella is a Latina; she is Caucasian, and she is his girlfriend. She is a successful businesswoman and an accountant. A bit arrogant.

She is tall and sensual with black hair and a ponytail. She doesn't know much about the supernatural, but she likes to go with her boyfriend, Jonas, everywhere and is always at the rituals.

Lou is black and wears glasses. He usually wears a scarf on his head. He practices Voodoo and Palo Mayombe.

Ella possesses an elegant, Caucasian appearance, with long hair and a light blonde complexion. She engages in necromantic practices, graveyard rituals, and general black magic.

This Coven exhibits a more Satanic nature.

The other secondary characters are Chloe, Victoria, Samuel, and Ralph.

Emma

Cedric

Evelyn

Jonas   Isabella   Penelope

Ella

Sorry for the quality of the drawings, it's just to give you an idea.

Chapter 1

In a world that walked closely with mythical possibilities, the Bombay Club stood as a haven of mystique in the heartbeat of New Orleans, an enigmatic realm nestled in the shadows of the city's history.
As it was known, the club was a haven for those who walked the line between light and darkness, where the mysteries of witchcraft, magic, and spirituality coalesced into a swirling dance of intrigue and danger.

The murmurs of patrons inside the club created a symphony of hushed conversations and laughter woven tightly into the club's existence.

At a corner table, beneath the soft glow of an amber-hued chandelier, sat Cedric, the leader of the Coven known as "Hidden Hand".
His features bore the essence of his world. His short, raven-black hair framed a countenance that carried the weight of both wisdom and an unquenchable thirst for knowledge. His fair skin contrasted aesthetically with his hair.

The talisman around his neck, an heirloom passed down through generations, rested proudly on his chest, its unique design glinting in the candlelight. His eyes, though fixed on the shifting currents of the room, seemed to reach beyond the veil of the mundane, as if he were attuned to the very pulse of the universe.

As the distant strains of a melancholic piano drifted through the air, Cedric's gaze shifted slowly around the interior of the Bombay Club. Finally, his eyes returned to the small crystal cup before him and he picked it up.

Cedric gulped down the last content of the glass and immediately followed with a prolonged sigh. He was out for a drink at the club.
It was a very popular and usually crowded club in New Orleans.

Emma, his girlfriend, was seated directly on the opposite side of his table.

"Want another one?" Emma asked, leaning in with her brows raised slightly.

"I think I'll take a break now," he replied. His voice carried a strange chill that Emma quickly associated with the gin he had just downed. It was winter and very cold outside, but the atmosphere inside the bar was welcoming. Almost cozy.

Emma continued staring at him with sharp and curious eyes. Her beauty was only surpassed by the fierce intelligence in her eyes. She had long, flowing brown hair that cascaded over her shoulders like a waterfall. Emma seemed to possess an otherworldly allure that drew others like moths to a light. They were sitting at the table, waiting for their friends.

Suddenly, Cedric sighted his old and former friend, Jonas. Announcing his presence with noisy strides from his boots, Jonas strolled into Bombay with his glamorous girlfriend, Isabella, next to him, Jonas heavily adorned chest making clunking sounds as his jewels danced against one another in the distance.

Cedric was soon queasy. "The atmosphere is already polluted," he said coldly, "I think I'll pass on that break and have another drink."

Emma pursed her lips together, her brows knitting in consternation. She turned around and searched for the always-moving waiter and signaled for another round of drinks. With a satisfied nod, the waiter acknowledged her and swiftly made his way toward the bar. Turning back to her boyfriend, Emma's eyes softened with a mix of concern and curiosity.

"Babe, you and Jonas were such good friends, explain to me what really happened? How did you come to hate each other so much?" Emma asked in a low voice.

The words hung in the air, a weighty question that seemed to demand an answer. Cedric's face tightened, his jaw clenching as if he were fighting back a torrent of emotions.

"Real friends don't stab each other in the back, spreading lies and saying they're better," Cedric said with an obvious and building anger in his tone as he spoke, "...Plus, in the past, he helped a relationship fall apart." He continued.

His gaze was distant, lost in the past that seemed to have etched itself deep into his memory.

Emma was still confused, and her expressions did nothing to hide it. She squeezed her brows as she spoke softly, "But what lies did he divulge?" She insisted, her words laced with a determination to unearth the truth.

"You know he also has a Coven, right?" Cedric asked.

Emma nodded, her gaze fixed on him, urging him to continue.

"It's called the 'Nightshadow Dew', and they think they are better than our Coven," said Cedric, his tone laced with a palpable disdain.

"Yes, but unfortunately, there is a lot of rivalry between Covens,". She remarked, her voice carrying a touch of sorrow. She knew all too well the complexities and tensions that could arise within the tightly-knit world of Covens, where differences and competition often led to fractures that ran deep.

As if on cue, the waiter reappeared, bearing a tray of drinks.

The clinking of glasses and the pleasant aroma of the concoctions filled the air, momentarily distracting them from the weight of their conversation.

"And his girlfriend Isabella, who thinks she's wisdom personified, also spreads shit about me in her magazines," Cedric continued, taking a swig of whiskey.

"Love, don't bother too much about these things. It's the price of being the leader of a famous Coven and an accomplished author who has published several books," Emma's features were passionate as she tried to ease him down. She simultaneously grabbed a Martini from the waiter's tray.

"I know, but these fanciful and rosy press articles...damage my image." Cedric pressed on. "I have clients and associates, and it's bad for business," said Cedric.

"I know, my love." Emma reached across and held his hand, rubbing gently at it.

Cedric couldn't help but take another look at Jonas and his girlfriend. They were already settled at the other end of the club. Jonas had a smirk permanently planted on his face.

He looked like a jerk from a distance, surrounded by a cloud of smoke from his Cuban cigar. The wispy veil of Cuban cigar smoke seemed to dance around him like a loyal companion, contributing to the air of arrogance that surrounded him. He kissed Isabella on the mouth as if he were showing off a trophy.

Cedric shook his head out of irritation as he turned back to Emma. "More than half of what he knows now he learned from me," Cedric said again. His fingers drummed restlessly against the rim of his glass, a manifestation of his internal turmoil.

"I was the one who introduced him to the occult, who guided him through the labyrinth of ancient texts and handed him the keys to forbidden knowledge," Cedric continued, his voice carrying a hint of bitterness that underscored his words.

"Now, after all these years, I stand as the leader of our Coven, and what does he do? He decides to fashion his own Coven, as if emulating my success is the path to his own glory."

He paused and went on again: "Not only that, he goes around saying he's wiser and more experienced than me. And his girlfriend calls me a fraud and a scammer in the magazines."

"Maybe we should sue them?" Emma suggested.

"I sued them once, but it didn't do much good," said Cedric, irritated.

"It doesn't matter," Emma said. "I believe in you, love, and I'm here by your side to listen and support you whenever you want." Emma sketched a shy but understanding smile after she'd said that to him. It warmed him up momentarily.

"Finally!" Cedric said. Their friends had just arrived. They sighted the couple immediately as they walked into the club— Leonard, Penelope, and Evelyn.

Evelyn spoke first: "Hi, everyone. Good evening." she said with a smile. Her dreadlocks, a cascade of intertwined obsidian strands lined with delicate streaks of light blue, framed a face that bore the imprints of innate depth. Evelyn's attire was an ensemble of flowing midnight hues and celestial patterns that seemed to shift and shimmer with the arcane currents coursing through the Bombay Club.
She had a pendant, a delicate sapphire suspended from a silver chain, nestled between her clavicles.

Her psychic abilities were renowned amongst the Coven, her mind was a conduit to dimensions beyond sight and sound. She has the ability of remote viewing; her consciousness was able to traverse the boundaries of space and time, peering into realms both seen and unseen. But for Evelyn herself, her gift of healing set her apart.

Everyone greeted each other with kisses.

"What do you want to drink?" Cedric asked them and motioned with his hand for the waiter.

"For me, a piña colada," said Evelyn.

"I'll take whiskey," Leonard said.

He was also a friend and member of their Coven. He had a vibrant shock of fiery red hair that seemed to dance with the very flames of the cosmos. Leonard's appearance was as striking as it was intriguing. His spiky hair, a testament to his free spirit and irreverent charm, held an air of casual defiance, a reflection of a soul unbound by convention.

He was always clad in a specific style of shirt, and seemed to have a perpetual array of them. Leonard had a strong connection to the Santería religion. The Hidden Hand Coven is not limited to a specific magical system. They practice different systems depending on their objectives.

14

"And I'll have just a gin," Penelope announced, her child-like personality warming up the rest of the group as usual.

Among the group, Penelope had a quiet personality with an air of quiet introspection and hidden desires. Her short, dark hair framed her countenance like a cascade of midnight silk, cascading in gentle waves that seemed to hold secrets whispered by the night itself. Behind the lenses of her glasses, her youthful eyes held a glimmer of depth, like windows to a soul that harbored complexities beyond mere sight.

As a practitioner of Wicca, Penelope held a connection to ancient traditions and mystical energies that flowed through the very veins of the earth. Her understanding of the delicate balance between nature, magic, and the human spirit added an important layer of depth to the Coven's dynamic.

Penelope had a hidden crush on Evelyn that the rest of the group noticed, yet the two appeared to be unaware of it.

She turned slightly and saw Jonas at the end of the room. "Look, isn't that the idiot Jonas over there?" Penelope asked the rest of the group.

"Don't even bring him up," Emma quickly said. "Cedric has already seen enough of him and was getting bored and angry as we waited for you guys," Emma added.

"Fucking satanic Coven," Evelyn mumbled under her breath with disdain. They all shared a common hatred for Jonas and his crew.

Emma Instantly saw the tense look building up on Cedric's face once again, so she said, "Let's dance a little, love, to clear your mind".

Welcoming the idea, Cedric decided it would do him more good than bad. "OK, let's go," he said with a quick nod, swallowing the last of his whiskey.

While the two danced, Isabella appeared on the small dance floor, swaying her hips sensually to the music. Jonas came hand in hand with her, with a cloud of smoke behind them. As Jonas's voice broke through the background melody, his teasing words hung in the air like a challenge:

"So you still have your esoteric shop? And the Coven? I thought they were over," Jonas said teasingly to Cedric, drewing on his cuban cigar.

Cedric's response was swift and laced with an underlying defiance. "Closed?

You're the one who will be left miserable when your clients realize they have more bad luck in life than benefits in getting involved with you," he retorted, the words dripping with a venomous truth that was as sharp as a blade. His gaze locked onto Jonas's, a challenge that dared him to consider the potency of his words.

"Babe, ignore them," Emma said. Her eyes beseeching Cedric to rise above the provocation.

On the other hand, Isabella just kept smiling with the air of someone who was having fun with the situation. But she said nothing. There was a tense atmosphere between Cedric and Jonas. If their eyes could emit lightning, there would certainly be a storm there.

"I saw in the cards that you're going to have a very unlucky year," Jonas said, his distasteful look intensifying the sting of his words. After that, he grabbed Isabella, and they slowly walked away.

Cedric stopped and shot Emma a sharp look. "What did that idiot mean by that?" He asked her as they walked back to their table.

As Cedric and Emma returned to the table, Evelyn pointed toward Jonas and Isabella on the other end and asked. "Did those suckers bother you?" She asked.

"It's what they do. Jonas kept on rambling about something along the line of us having a very bad year with luck," Cedric replied dryly.

Evelyn could tell that what he'd just heard from Jonas had slightly disturbed him.

"Don't listen to him for a second. He's just jealous of what you have. We are strong, united and no bad omen can ever bring us down," Evelyn said affirmatively, trying her best to reassure their leader.

"I'm going to the bathroom. I'll be right back,". Evelyn told the group, getting up from the table.

Penelope hurried up to her instantly. "Wait, I'll keep you company," she called after Evelyn. Emma smiled and gave Cedric a knowing look.

Penelope heard, but she ignored them and continued after Evelyn. She caught up with her before she got too far away.

"Ah," Evelyn exclaimed as she turned around, "Do you really need to come to the bathroom with me?" She asked curiously.

"I'll be back in no time." She added.

"Well…I wanted to talk to you," Penelope said, "Away from the group." Her shy smile made her look even more like a child.

Evelyn couldn't help herself. Penelope had such an effect on people whenever she smiled. She grinned at Penelope's blushing sight.

"What do you wanna say, Penelope?" She asked softly, almost as though she was whispering.

"Well, Evelyn, I admire you a lot," Penelope started. Adjusting her glasses.

"Thank you," Evelyn said. "But can I ask specifically why that is, Penelope?" Evelyn asked in a different tone.

"Well, I guess I just wanna tell you how much I admire you for having the courage to do what you did, taking up yourself as you want to be— as a woman, we all know your story because you shared it with us. You made the transition to be a woman and you were successful. That's courage." Penelope said. She already found herself stroking Evelyn's hair, caressing the part of the locks with some shades of light blue.

"Ah, thanks," Evelyn said, feeling a little uncomfortable.

"And…" continued Penelope, "I…Uh…You know…" She stammered, dropping her head down.

"What is it, Penelope?" Evelyn inquired.

"Okay," she looked up again, seemingly summoning more courage as she sighed deeply. "I just want you to know that…uh…I'm actually attracted to women." Penelope told her, and she dropped her head into a bow once again.

"I know," Evelyn said. She touched Penelope's chin and raised her head slowly until their eyes met. She continued, "...And that's also courageous to admit to the world without fear," Evelyn continued. "But I've always felt like a woman, and now I'm a woman, but the truth is... I'm interested in men," she told her calmly, not trying to hurt her feelings.

"Yes, I understand, but..." Penelope started, but she was cut off.

"Do you understand what I'm trying to say? I know you came to me hoping I wasn't like that, but that's how it is with me," Evelyn admitted.

The look on Penelope's face showed her huge disappointment. Since the very first time she'd met Evelyn, she'd had a soft spot in her heart for her. She would steal glances at her whenever they were all together.

Right now, as Evelyn told her she wasn't interested in girls, Penelope realized she had much more than a mere crush on her. Her heart squeezed, and felt like as if something was twisting harshly inside her.

"But Evelyn, we still can..." Penelope said, trailing off.

"Come on, don't insist, okay?" Evelyn spoke gently, disguising her discomfort with a forced smile and patting her shoulder.

Penelope opened her mouth and spoke softly, "I have to admit. Right now, I want to kiss you on the mouth and find out if you would like it, but I respect your preferences and won't insist further." Penelope said.

"Of course, don't worry; hold my bag, please. I'm going to pee," said Evelyn.

"Okay, I'll wait here for you."

After a while, Evelyn was back. Then the two returned to the table.

"Women always go to the toilet in pairs. Why is that?" Leonard asked with a naughty smile.

"You've got some real sense in your head, Leonard," Evelyn said sarcastically.

"Look, the suckers are leaving," Cedric said, looking towards Jonas and Isabella.

"You can breathe better now," Emma added with conviction.

The group spent more time together in the club, and at the end of the night, they left and said their goodbyes.

"It was a good time, guys. See you tomorrow and rest well," said Cedric as he got into the car with Emma.

Chapter 2

The next morning's sunlight streamed gently through the curtains, casting a warm glow across the room. However, as Emma stirred from her slumber, she was immediately aware that something was amiss. Her body felt numb, and she was shaking all over as though she'd been exposed to an intensely cold temperature. The sensation of numbness, like a veil enveloping her, left her feeling disconnected from her own limbs.

As the disconcerting feeling took hold, Cedric's voice cut through the haze of her discomfort. Concern etched lines onto his face as he hovered over her, his worry was noticeable.

"What is going on, babe. Are you okay?" He inquired, his voice tinged with a mixture of confusion and alarm. His fingers brushed against her arm gently, seeking to offer reassurance even as he grappled with his own uncertainty.

Emma's response was a tremulous admission of her own confusion. "I don't know what's happening to me," she managed to articulate, her voice carrying a hint of helplessness.

"I feel strange. My body feels strange—hot and cold at the same time." Her words wavered as the sensation persisted— a bizarre juxtaposition of sensations that left her feeling utterly off-kilter.

"I don't understand. Did something happen?"

"Ah! My head is killing me!" She exclaimed, her voice laced with anguish as her hands instinctively moved to calm her throbbing temples.

In a disconcerting twist of events, Emma's body began to writhe, her movements erratic and uncontrollable. Just as abruptly as it began, her wriggling ceased, her head lifting as if drawn by some unseen force. A voice, deeper and altogether unfamiliar, emerged from her lips, its timbre carrying an otherworldly resonance.

"I bring a message," Her voice had deepened beyond the usual. It wasn't hers. Something else spoke through her. Cedric realized she'd had embodiment mediumship taken over her.

"Some deaths will happen!" The proclamation echoed through the room, its weighty words hanging in the air like a premonition.

Emma's eyes rolled back, and then she fainted.

Then, as if the strange presence had concluded its message, her body sagged, her consciousness seemingly slipping away. With swift reflexes, Cedric moved to catch her, his arms enveloping her form just in time to prevent her from collapsing onto the bed.

"Babe? Can you hear me? Wake up. Emma?" Cedric said in quick succession. His heart was beating quickly as he patted her face gently, hoping to get a response from her inactive body.

After a short while, Emma woke up again.

She took a deep breath; her demeanor calmer, and her eyes focused on Cedric.

- "What happened?" She inquired, her voice carrying a fragility that mirrored the aftermath of the profound experience that had seized her.

Cedric was blunt. "You incorporated a spirit," he explained. "I don't know which one because he didn't identify himself but spoke of deaths."

"Deaths?" Emma was still recovering, but she was visibly shocked by what she'd just heard. Her voice wavered with a blend of curiosity and shock. The gravity of the message seemed to hang in the air, casting a shadow over the room.

Cedric nodded solemnly, confirming her question. "Yes," he confirmed, his gaze unwavering as he met her eyes.

With a determined resolve, Emma shifted her position, pushing herself into a sitting position on the bed. The tarot deck, her tool for seeking

22

insights, lay within arm's reach, and she reached for it.
"I'm going to read the tarot cards," she stated, her voice holding a note of both intention and urgency.

As the cards were spread before her, their enigmatic images began to weave a narrative that would offer insight into the events that had transpired.

As the cards were laid out, a trio of unsettling images revealed themselves: The Devil, The Tower, and Death. Emma's reaction was visceral, with a sharp exhalation escaping her lips as she cussed under her breath.

"Shit," she muttered, her fingers brushing over the cards as if seeking answers within their intricate designs. "Just negative cards.
Someone has done macumba against us," she concluded, her words laden with a weight of hurt and a hint of anger.

"So many negative cards together is unusual,". He mused, his voice carrying a somber acknowledgment of the rarity of this alignment.
The realization that someone had directed ill intentions their way weighed heavily on them both.

For a moment, there was a heavy silence. The challenge before them was clear, and together, they were determined to navigate the currents of uncertainty and adversity that had been set in motion.

Shortly after, Cedric's cell phone rings, breaking the silence. It was his friend, Leonard.

Leonard's voice sounded urgent and serious, in sync with the current situation on their side of the call. "Cedric," Leonard stated, "I had a bad feeling, and today I assure you that in my house I saw some black figures. I don't think they were hallucinations!" He said.

Cedric's brows furrowed as he processed the information, his own concerns aligning with Leonard's experience.

"I believe you," he responded without hesitation, his voice carrying a shared sense of gravity. "Something is wrong,"
Cedric continued, his words tinged with a mix of uncertainty and conviction. "Just not long ago, Emma felt sick, and a spirit took over her body and spoke through her," he explained, his voice heavy with

23

the weight of the unusual occurrence. "This usually happens only in incorporation rituals and definitely only under her will.
But this time it was awkward and out of control. It sent a negative message to us."

Cedric explained it to his friend.

The gravity of the situation seemed to be magnified as the words crossed the distance through the phone call. On the other end, Leonard's response was succinct, carrying an acknowledgement of the brewing trouble. "Oh... someone must have done shit to us," he muttered, his voice reflecting a mixture of frustration and concern.

Cedric's frustration was palpable as he continued to recount the unfolding events.

"No shit! And there's more!" He exclaimed, the edge in his voice revealing the tension he was grappling with. "Emma saw Death, the Tower, and the Devil in the cards... Just fucking bad cards only..." He sighed, a mixture of disbelief and frustration evident in his tone.

"Emma kept throwing the cards, and there was always Death, the Devil, the Tower, then the Hanged Man..." His voice trailed off, the weight of their situation echoing through the phone call.

There was a noticeable pause in the call between the two of them. The two of them were absorbing what was happening and what the other had just shared, and they were figuring out the next steps.

"Let's get the Coven together," Cedric suggested as the obvious next course of action.

"I'll call Penelope, Zoey, John, Wilbur, and everyone else." He informed his friend.

"Yes love, let's do that," agreed Emma, nodding affirmatively and still shaken from what had happened to her.

"Leonard, can you stop by the esoteric store and pick up Evelyn? Meet us at the Coven temple."

"OK."

They end up the call and went to action.

About half an hour later, they were all gathered: Cedric, Emma, Zoey, John, Wilbur, Leonard, Evelyn, and others arrived. Penelope arrived late and looked worried. Each face carrying a mixture of curiosity and concern.

"Listen carefully, guys." Cedric started with the group, his voice urgent and carrying the weight of the situation. "Something is wrong, and I think someone wants to harm us," Cedric told them.

Evelyn, known for her psychic abilities and her capacity for remote viewing, remained silent, her eyes distant as if she were gazing into a realm beyond their own. The rest of the Coven members sensed her introspection and turned their attention to her, their collective curiosity piqued.

Suddenly, Evelyn's voice broke through the silence, her words carrying a quiet but certain authority. "On this," she began, her voice steady as she emerged from her vision. "It was Jonas' Coven, the 'Nightshadow Dew'," she continued, her words painting a vivid picture of the events she had witnessed.

"I just had a vision of them. They did a ritual last night, and when Jonas and Isabella left the bar, they went to join the rest of the group who were already doing a ritual in the woods."

" Cedric's nerves seemed to ratchet up a notch as the pieces of the puzzle fell into place. "Sons of bitches, I knew they were up to something," he muttered, his words tinged with a mixture of frustration and a gnawing unease. The realization that the threat they faced was not just happenstance but an orchestrated effort by a rival Coven cast a shadow over the room.

"Fuckers!" Emma's voice cut through the tension, her response marked by a heavy look that mirrored the emotions swirling within her. Her gaze hardened, a mix of anger and determination flickering in her eyes.

25

In that moment, as the Coven members sat encircled by the unknown and the unsettling, a silent pact seemed to form among them. The threads of unity and purpose were woven ever tighter as they prepared to confront the darkness that encroached upon their world.

"We're not going to stand idly by with crossed arms because of karma and all, are we?" Leonard asked.

"Crossed arms? They played with fire, and now they get burned." Emma said.

"I agree," Penelope cut in.

"When something challenges you, you have three options," Cedric said with a raised voice. He sounded more fierce and angry. "You either let it challenge you, destroy you, or make you stronger," said Cedric. "And this will make us stronger. That's how we must treat it."

"Guys, let's place a very heavy curse on them tonight... While you do the ritual, I'll visualize their faces and psychically direct the energy of the ritual to them. What do you think?" Evelyn asked.

"Good idea," Cedric said. They all concluded and reached an agreement.

They all left the temple in their vehicles, in agreement to return later at night for the rituals. The rituals have specific magical hours, and night is the ideal time.

By eleven at night, they were all gathered in the temple.

"Is everybody here?" Asked Cedric.

As the conversation hung in the air, an unexpected entrance shattered the gathering's uneasy equilibrium. Penelope, her eyes swollen from crying and her face etched with distress, appeared at the doorway. The rawness of her emotions was palpable; the tears that streamed down her cheeks painting a picture of turmoil and anguish.

Leonard was the first to react; his concern was immediate and evident. "What is it, Penelope?" He asked with imperativeness, his voice a reflection of the urgency that accompanied her emotional state.

Cedric, equally worried, echoed the question - "What happened?" He insisted, his gaze fixed on Penelope's trembling figure.

Overwhelmed by the weight of her emotions, Penelope collapsed to the floor, her sobs escaping in uncontrollable waves. For a moment, her voice was lost in her anguish, leaving the room in a heavy silence punctuated only by her tears.

As her cries gradually subsided, Penelope found her voice shaky and laden with sorrow. With a deep breath, she addressed the group, her words carrying a heaviness that mirrored her emotions. "John and Wilbur had a car accident on the way home," she began, the tremor in her voice reflecting the gravity of the situation.

"I think the car fell off the Crescent City Bridge. I don't know if they survived," she concluded, her words trailing off in a painful admission of uncertainty.

The room seemed to collectively hold its breath as Penelope's words sank in.

"Oh my!" Leonard exclaimed. His shock and worry mirroring the sentiments of the others.

Cedric's reaction was visceral, a mixture of disbelief and frustration that he couldn't quite contain. "Damn!" He muttered, his jaw clenching as he averted his gaze, as if needing a moment to grapple with the news. He walked away from the group, distancing himself from the intensity of the moment and allowing the reality of their situation to settle in.

"Fuck! This is getting really bad!" Emma exclaimed, her frustration and concern manifesting in her tone. The weight of the escalating events was a heavy burden that seemed to press upon them all.

Instantly, Evelyn started meditating, her eyes closed as she sought to connect with a deeper understanding of the events that had unfolded.

As Cedric returned to the core of the Coven, his determination was palpable.
"Let's do the ritual," his words rang out with a sense of unwavering

purpose. His resolve seemed to spread like wildfire, igniting a collective determination among the members who were present.

Without hesitation, the Coven members sprang into action, the urgency in the air driving them to swift and decisive movements. There was no room for hesitation after Penelope had just delivered the devastating news. They were united in their resolve to confront the threat that loomed over them, to push back against the forces that sought to harm their Coven.

They lit black candles and placed offerings such as bottles of whiskey, black candles, and four-legged animals to sacrifice.

As the Coven members assumed their positions, their voices rose in unison, creating a powerful chorus that reverberated through the room. "We invoke Papa Legba and his brother Met Kalfu to open our paths!"

Their voices rang out, charged with energy and purpose, and their arms were raised in a gesture that reached towards the spiritual realms.

"We invoke Baron Samedi, lord and ruler of the world of the dead, to bring the curse to our enemies!" They continued as Cedric held a skull in his hands. It was real, and it belonged to an actual person. They had their ways of getting things like this.

The chanting continued, "We invoke your companion Maman Brigitte, queen of cemeteries, wife of Baron Samedi, to punish those who wanted to hurt us.". He intoned, his gaze fixed upon the skull as if seeking a connection to the spirits they invoked.

As the ritual progressed, a primal energy seemed to fill the room. Drums were brought forth, their rhythms building like a thunderous heartbeat. The atmosphere grew charged as the time for sacrifice approached. When the moment was right, the members of the Coven began to beat the drums with a fervor that matched the intensity of their intent.

The culmination of the ritual arrived, marked by the sacrifice of the animals. Their blood was spilled over pictures of their rivals from the Nightshadow Dew Coven, a symbolic act that bound their intentions to the physical world. The room seemed to vibrate with the convergence of energies -- a potent mixture of determination, power, and a touch of the unknown.

After it was all done, their faces all began to carry looks of satisfaction. "The offerings have been made, and now the loa will respond and come to our aid," said Cedric, confidently.

As the ritual came to an end, a palpable sense of unity and purpose lingered in the air. The members of the Coven knew that they had sent a message, both to the spiritual forces they invoked and to the enemies that had dared to threaten their sanctuary. In that moment, their Coven was more than just a gathering of individuals – it was a united front against the darkness that sought to engulf them.

Evelyn continued with her eyes closed, concentrating and visualizing their enemies suffering a thousand storms as she psychically directed her energy toward them.

Suddenly, a loud noise sounded out of nowhere. It was like an explosion. All the glass windows shattered into a thousand pieces, and everyone momentarily tried to take cover.

"Damn! What the fuck is this?!" Cedric asked, his words directed at no one in particular.

Little did Cedric and the rest of the Hidden Hand Coven know that at exactly the same time their ritual was being carried out, Jonas and his Coven were also performing their own rites in Baton Rouge.

"I can feel some negative entities around here. It seems those suckers are fighting back," Jonas quickly said. "But we also know how to work with these entities or any other ones." He continued.

"We can do some curses and rituals with Eshús, I have experience in Palo Mayombe, and you know that Jonas..." One of them, known as Lou, said.

"Yes, my friend, those seem to be exactly what we need to do. I'm sure they are the right ones, but let's wait for Ella to return from the cemetery with some earth and bones." Jonas' voice went cold as he said that. He relished the idea of what they were about to do.

Isabela watched silently, with a look of excitement and malice.

"Man, I don't think I'm feeling well," Lou suddenly said.

"What do you mean?"

Lou instantly fell to his knees. A couple of Coven members rushed to grab him, but he'd started vomiting blood before anyone could get to him.

"Shit! I see what's happening now. Those fuckers are also up to something. They know what they are doing. It seems I've underestimated them more than I should." Jonas said.

"Cariño, let's take him to the hospital immediately," said Isabella.

"Samuel helps out here," Jonas added. And the two carried Lou in their arms and headed toward the car to take him to the hospital. "We'll be right behind you," he told them.

"This is going too far," Ralph said as they prepared to follow them to the hospital. "I don't want to lose my friends."

"That's why we can't stop now. We have to take revenge on those "Hidden Hand" shitholes," Isabella pressed.

"I know, but now it really hurts," said Jonas. "Having members of my Coven attacked like this."

"But who started it? It was us," Ralph said, looking a little wary and unsure whether he should have said what he just said. He blinked nervously as he looked at Jonas and Isabella for their reactions.

"Shut up! Now is not the time to have a crisis of conscience." Jonas retorted. "There is no such thing as good or evil, only circumstances."

"I know, but not if we're also losing our men, Jonas," Ralph pleaded, hoping to convince his leader. Somehow, he knew it was a waste of time, and Isabella could only give Jonas a change of heart. But as it stood, she was behind him, stronger than ever.

Tension was rising among the Coven as Jonas stared at Lou. It was quickly cut off as they heard a shout from the two taking Lou to the hospital.

"Lou!" Samuel's voice was loud as a wail as he shouted.

Jonas ran towards them immediately, and the rest of the Coven, including Isabella, followed.

"Let's rush him to the hospital now!"

They all hurried into different cars and drove off in three of them. Jonas and Ralph were both in the same car with Lou, and Samuel drove the car. Isabella stayed behind with some other female members of the Coven.

"Move quickly!" Ralph urged Samuel every second as they headed to the hospital. They were just about to arrive at the hospital with Lou when he collapsed.

"Lou!" Ralph screamed at the top of his voice. Lou gasped for breath and reached out his hand before he released his last breath with blood dripping from his mouth.

"Fuck you, Lou! Don't do that; don't die..." Ralph rambles in pain as he sees his friend dying. Tears gushed down from his eyes down his cheeks.

Jonas shook his head and bowed, notably shaken.

Ralph turned to Jonas and said, "People are dying, Jonas. This is getting serious. People are fucking dying!"

Jonas didn't even respond, trying to disguise the emptiness he felt. Nurses approached the car with a gurney. They took the body inside, but they all knew it was over. Lou was dead. They had just lost a very important friend and member of their Coven.

Jonas' cell phone rings. He picked it up and saw that it was Isabella. Jonas told her the sad news.

"Oh dear," Isabella said, "We lost our friend, Lou." She added in a sad voice.

Chapter 3

The next day, in the newspaper, everyone saw the news, including everyone in the Hidden Hand Coven.

"I can't believe that John and Wilbour really died," said Penelope, wearing a bitter expression on her face.

After she had come to the Coven with the news yesterday, they later went to find out what really happened, and their bodies had been found on the riverbank.

All the members hugged each other with sad and heavy hearts. Cedric, Emma, Leonard, Evelyn, and the rest of the Coven were present. It was a sad day for the Coven, losing two members. They were all so angry at Jonas and his Coven for doing this to them. But right now, they consoled one another for their loss.

"Look, it looks like Lou, a member of the Jonas Coven, also died," Cedric said to his girlfriend, Emma. He held the newspaper and related it to her.

"Seriously?" Emma asked. "And from our Coven, it was Wilbour and John in a strange car accident; it can't be a coincidence," Emma said with an air of concern.

"Ah, but they were the ones who started it, and we must continue to overthrow them at all costs, or some more of us may die, including you and me!" Cedric said.

"But..." Said Emma, but Cedric interrupted her before she could get more words out.

"But what? What if something happens to more of us, including me or you? I don't want to lose you, babe," Cedric said. "Nor do I want to lose any more members of this Coven."

"I understand," Emma said. "Well, honey, I'm going to work at the shop," Emma said, leaving. She had a cartomancy and spiritual counseling office in their esoteric shop.

"Okay, love, I'm also going to the Coven temple," Cedric added, his words revealing his own destination for the day. With a sense of purpose, he prepared himself for the journey ahead.

The journey took about 15 minutes by car. Upon arriving at the place, Cedric saw black candles, black chickens, and blood spilled at the doors of his temple.

Cedric's frustration bubbled to the surface, his irritation evident in his words. "Oh, now fuck them," he muttered under his breath, his tone a mixture of exasperation and indignation.
"This can already be considered vandalism, I'm going to file a complaint." He decided firmly, his resolve unwavering as he reached for his cell phone.

He called the police and filed a complaint.

After forty minutes, two agents were on the scene, collecting evidence. Cedric watched as they meticulously collected evidence, the gravity of the situation becoming more apparent with each passing moment.

"It seems you have made some enemies, Mr. Cedric," one of the agents remarked, their tone a mix of professional curiosity and sympathy. "Do you have any suspicions about who might have done this?" They inquired, their gaze fixed on Cedric as if seeking insight into the motive behind the act.

Cedric's mind raced, considering his response carefully. If he were to reveal the full extent of his suspicions and rivals, it could lead to further complications and questions. He decided on a measured approach.

"Well, you know, Mr. Agent, I have an esoteric shop and a religious cult, so normally I have competition, opponents, let's say," he explained, his words carrying a tone of nonchalance that masked the deeper tensions at play.

"I understand," Agent Curtis acknowledged, his expression thoughtful as he processed Cedric's explanation. "This can set up an act of property vandalism and crime against animals," he continued, his voice carrying a professional weight.

"But you can't file a complaint against strangers, can you? So do you have any suspicions?" he probed further, seeking to uncover any leads that might aid their investigation.

Cedric considered his response carefully, his thoughts racing to find a balance between transparency and discretion. "Perhaps another occult group?" he suggested, his tone tinged with a hint of curiosity.

"There's a well-known Coven called Nightshadow Dew, for example," he offered, his words carefully chosen to appear as though he were sharing information without revealing too much of his own knowledge.

"Okay," the agent nodded, his expression serious. "Let's investigate," he concluded, his words carrying a sense of determination. As the agents began their work, Cedric was left to grapple with the unsettling realization that the tensions within the occult community had escalated into tangible acts of vandalism and confrontation.

"Oh! Mr. Cedric, we are also investigating the car accident involving your friends Wilbour and John," the agent added.

"Investigating? But wasn't it a terrible accident?" Cedric asked, his tone marked by a mixture of confusion and concern. The assumption had been that the incident was a tragic but unfortunate mishap on the road.

"We're investigating, Mr. Cedric," agent Curtis confirmed, his words accompanied by a nod from his colleague. "After reading the first reports, we have concluded that the circumstances surrounding the accident aren't clear enough to rule it outright as an accident."

A frown quickly appeared on Cedric's face. Of course, he knew it wasn't an accident. Jonas and his Coven had done some evil magic to bring about the accident, but he was surprised that the police also knew that. He decided to find out exactly what they knew.

"I don't understand, agent " he said, looking genuinely confused. "What do you mean the circumstances surrounding the accident aren't clear?"

The agent's response was clinical, his words revealing a deeper analysis that had been carried out. "Autopsy reports came out, and the two victims, most importantly the driver, were perfectly healthy prior to the accident. They weren't at a bend, and forensics said that they didn't seem to be speeding, given how the impact of their landing was.

So we are left wondering. How could they have swerved so acutely when it wasn't a health-related problem or reckless driving?"

The realization dawned on Cedric. The police were piecing together the puzzle, and while they may not have all the answers, their investigation was starting to connect the dots. Jonas and his coven's involvement was becoming evident, even to those outside the occult world.
Maintaining his pretense of confusion, Cedric let out a contemplative sigh.

"I see your point, Agent. So what do you think really happened, and what can we do about it?" he inquired, his words laced with a sense of both curiosity and concern.

"Well... You've got to leave that to us," agent Curtis responded, his tone carrying a note of professional reassurance. "We'll continue our investigation and let you know if there's any new development that you need to know."

"Alright, agents. Thank you for your time." He thanked them, and they departed.

Cedric couldn't help but wonder if the police were up to something. They might not be into witchcraft and the like, but the police weren't fools. He looked forward to seeing what would unfold next.

Back at home, Emma played the cards again— Death, the Devil, and the Tower continued to appear, all bad omens. The Devil meant hidden enemies and bad influences, but also some habit or feeling of resentment that imprisoned them.

The Tower meant that something was going to fall apart, and everything seemed to be falling apart. It might rise again, but it will take a long time. Death doesn't always mean "death". It can mean something ending suddenly, something changing a lot, or someone getting sick. But the truth is that people have already died— Wilbour and John from their Coven and Lou from the other side.

Emma retreated into a state of trance, her eyes twitching.

Cedric, his concern evident in his furrowed brows and the tight grip with which he held her, watched her with a mixture of worry and care.

"Again, babe?" Cedric's voice carried a note of tender concern; his words were laced with a genuine desire to understand and support her. As her body shook in what seemed like spasms, he held her close, his embrace a reassuring anchor amidst the tumultuous currents that seemed to be coursing through her.

Within the depths of her trance, a voice emerged, its resonance thick and layered, like the convergence of several entities speaking in unison. The metallic tone that echoed forth created an eerie symphony, as if the words themselves were being drawn from the depths of some metallic tunnel.

"This war between your Covens was decided on the spiritual plane long before," the voice declared, its words carrying a weight that resonated with ancient authority. "
A war between the entities that govern you, and that spiritual war between entities has extended to you.

"Who are you? What is your name? Are you trying to advise us to help, or are you one of those negative entities?"
Cedric's words tumbled forth in rapid succession, his voice a mix of urgency and determination. The need to understand the nature of this entity and its intentions was paramount for the safety of their coven and the balance of their spiritual realm.

But as quickly as the entity had emerged, it retreated, its presence vanishing into the ethereal shadows. Emma's trance dissipated, her eyes fluttering open as she returned to the realm of the living.

"I feel dizzy," she admitted, her voice carrying the residue of her encounter with the enigmatic force. "I think I have a headache."

Cedric nodded, his gaze fixed on her with a mixture of relief and curiosity. "You were gone again.". He told her, the words carrying a weight of both observation and concern.

"I don't remember what happened. I went back to channeling that entity, didn't I?" Emma's question hung in the air, her uncertainty mirroring the complexity of the situation. Her heart raced with a mixture of anxiety and a thirst for understanding.

"Yes, the entity says that this war started on the spiritual plane and that we are all being manipulated by rival spirits between Covens, I think.". Said Cedric.

"I'll call Evelyn and Penelope; I'll have coffee with them and tell them everything. Maybe they can help and tell me their point of view," Emma told him.

"Good idea. Will you be okay? What can I get you?". He asked.

"I'll be fine. It's happened before, and I don't think this will be the last time. We need to find a way to understand what's going on. Just water will be okay for now," Emma told Cedric.

"Okay. I'll get you water."

Later at the Mammoth Expresso cafe, Evelyn was already waiting for Emma at a table. Emma called her and Penelope to meet up at the cafe.

"So Penelope?" Emma asked, carrying a note of curiosity.

Evelyn's response held a hint of reservation. "Oh, she said she couldn't come," she revealed, her tone accompanied by a subtle shift in her expression.
"You know, I don't have a good feeling about her," she continued, her words unfolding with a mixture of candor and unease.
"I don't know, but I feel like I can't trust her, and sometimes I try to get visions about her and find out more, but nothing comes up. Still, I get this kind of bad vibe when it comes to her.".

"Hmmm, do you think she cannot be trusted?" Emma mused aloud, her intrigue evident as she sought to grasp the intricacies of Evelyn's instincts.

"I don't know, Emma," Evelyn admitted, with a mixture of uncertainty and frustration.

"Anyways, she's not here now," Emma stated matter-of-factly, her tone shifting to one of focus and seriousness. She leaned forward slightly, her gaze locked onto Evelyn's.

"You know, today, I channeled that entity again," she began, her voice lowering as if sharing a secret. "The spirit said that this war between the Covens started on the spiritual plane and that we are being manipulated."

The revelation caused Evelyn's eyes to slightly widen, piqued her interest. She leaned in, absorbing Emma's words with a mixture of curiosity and contemplation.

"Is that even possible?" She questioned, her tone tinged with a blend of wonder.

"Could these dark spirits have attacked us directly?" Evelyn posed another question, her thoughts clearly racing as she tried to piece together the puzzle of their predicament.

"I'm trying to figure that out," Emma admitted with a sigh, her fingers tracing a pattern on the tabletop as if searching for answers. "But on the other hand, Jonas threatened us at the bar, so it's natural that he followed that threat up with a spiritual attack." She speculated, her voice reflecting the uncertainty that colored her thoughts.

"But then, according to what the spirit tried to tell us, it could all be under the influence of those spirits, you see," Evelyn said.

"Yes, maybe," Emma agreed. "But we know nothing for certain for now. I just needed to tell you guys so we could all know what to be digging for. People are dying, and we can't allow that to continue."

"You're right. We should consider all possibilities. I'll be on it, I promise."

When Emma returned to the house, she saw that Cedric had lit some candles on his altar for the Loa to provide protection. Emma came back and met him in the middle of it.

The conversation with Evelyn echoed in her thoughts as she proceeded to recount it to Cedric, her voice carrying the blend of uncertainty and concern that had marked their exchange.

"Penelope didn't show up, and Evelyn thinks she can't be trusted," Emma summarized, her words laced with a mixture of contemplation and caution.

Cedric's surprise was evident as he absorbed the information. "Seriously?" he responded, his tone reflecting his own astonishment at the notion. After a moment of consideration, he conceded, "Well, I know little about her, really".

Emma's gaze held a mixture of earnestness and a plea for understanding. "Honey, if we're all being influenced by spirits like puppets in a game, maybe you could try talking to Jonas," she suggested, her voice imbued with a pleading urgency.
"We could avoid more people dying on both sides," she added, the gravity of their situation giving her words a weight that resonated deeply.

There was a long pause before Cedric replied.

"I'll try," he said. His tone was a mixture of determination and the weight of responsibility.

"Do you still have his number?" Emma asked.

"No, but I'll ask a boy we know in common, Miguel," Cedric replied, his willingness to reach out to Jonas evident in his response.

"Ok. Good," Emma acknowledged, the tension in her features giving way to a glimmer of relief.

In the midst of their contemplation, Cedric's cell phone rang, the call unexpected yet not entirely surprising. It was the police detective, agent Curtis, on the line, his voice carrying a seriousness that cut through the air.

Cedric's mind raced, the gravity of the situation settling over him like a heavy shroud. "Thank you, Agent Curtis," he responded after a moment of contemplation. "

Continue to inform me of the situation depending on what you find out," he added, his voice carrying a mix of gratitude and an underlying demand for answers.

As the call ended, the weight of their reality hung heavy in the air, the convergence of the spiritual and the tangible creating a tapestry of uncertainty that stretched out before them. In the quiet space of their home, surrounded by the gentle glow of candles, Cedric and Emma shared a look that spoke volumes—a silent affirmation of their resolve to navigate the stormy seas that lay ahead.

Chapter 4

That night, Cedric met Jonas at the Bombay Club. He'd called him as soon as he got his number from Miguel. Jonas had first sounded like his usual self over the call, trying to be a jerk. But when he realized that Cedric was serious about the meeting, he began to see things differently, so they eventually agreed to meet at the Bombay Club.

As the two faced each other across the table, their gazes locked in a silent battle of wills, the jazz melodies that wafted through the air seemed to underscore the tension between them. Cedric's determination was palpable, a resolve that transcended their animosity, while Jonas's arrogance was worn like armor, a facade he wielded with calculated finesse.

"So, what did you want to talk about? You know I don't like you very much," Jonas said in an arrogant tone, speaking louder than the jazz music in the background.

"Well, I don't sympathize with you either", he retorted, his tone measured and direct. "But have you noticed that people have died on both sides now?" He asked, his words cutting through the superficial veneer that often masked their interactions.
"For what? Have you actually taken time to consider what exactly is going on?"

Jonas's initial bravado wavered, his expression shifting as the gravity of Cedric's words began to seep into his consciousness. "What do you mean? I know what's going on," he replied, a hint of defensiveness creeping into his tone.
"You're jealous of what I've achieved with my Coven, without your help. And you intend to bring us down.

That's exactly what's going on between us," he added, punctuating his words with a wild, self-satisfying smile that hovered on the edge of arrogance.

Cedric's gaze remained unyielding, a mirror to the complexities that ran beneath the surface of their rivalry. "I know you lack the depth of understanding and discernment," he began, his voice steady even as he acknowledged their differences.

"But I'll say this again for the sake of your people and mine. Consider why I would be coming here to meet you if there isn't an element of strangeness in what is going on?"

The seed of doubt seemed to find fertile ground within Jonas's mind — a flicker of uncertainty that danced across his features. "Hmm… what are you driving at?" he asked, his arrogance momentarily quelled by a sense of curiosity.

Cedric seized the opportunity, his voice carrying a mixture of urgency and sincerity. "I think both our Covens are being manipulated by some dark spirits," he declared, his words heavy with the weight of a revelation that transcended their animosity.

"Do you want evil to come to you and Isabella?" He asked pointedly. "I don't want it to get to me or Emma, so we've got to do something about it".

Jonas laughed loudly and said, "I want you to fuck off. I don't give a damn. Is that all you wanted to talk about?
Truces?" Jonas said. He retorted, his voice crackling like a whip in the air. His bravado returned, his armor reforged, as he dismissed Cedric's words with brazen defiance.

"I see; I can't talk to you. It was a mistake," admitted Cedric.

"Yeah, I think it was," Jonas said, getting up.

"The police are investigating; it seems that our friend's car was sabotaged. I thought you guys only did witchcraft? Do you also sabotage vehicles and murder people?" asked Cedric.

"We have nothing to do with this," Jonas said. And he left.

Cedric tried to follow him, hoping to drop a last word and hurt his ego. Then he quickly noticed that Jonas had met a girl at the end of the street. He moved closer and found out that the girl was Penelope.

"But why does this bitch talk to him?" Cedric wondered.

Immediately, without hesitating, he called Emma, who was already home.

"Love," he started, "the conversation didn't go well. With the shitty attitude that Jonas has, you already know, but imagine who I saw talking to him on the street? " Asked Cedric.

"Who?" asked Emma on the other end of the line, curious.

"Penelope," Cedric said, dropping the bombshell.

"Oh, yes? Well, Evelyn said she didn't trust her very much. I guess I shouldn't be surprised," said Emma.

Cedric turned and saw Penelope get into Jonas's car.

"Look, she got into his car!" He said.

"Seriously? I can't believe this girl betrayed us," Emma said, sounding genuinely disappointed.

"I'll meet you at home soon, love. I'm on my way," said Cedric.

Arriving home, Cedric heard the sound of the shower water. Emma was taking a shower. He decided to join her.

Emma blushed as she saw him come into the shower.

Cedric teased her: "We're going to rub that little body of yours with a flushing bath with magical herbs to purify and provide protection," Cedric said.

"Good idea," Emma said, smiling and embracing him tightly in the bath.

The next day, Emma met Evelyn, and they decided to look for Penelope.

"You know where she works, right?" Asked Emma.

"Yes, over there at the library," Evelyn said.

"Let's wait here on the street. It's almost time for her to close. It's 5:30 p.m.; let's wait a bit." Emma said.

After about five minutes, they caught a glimpse of Penelope walking out the library door.

"Let's follow her and see where she's headed," Evelyn suggested.

"Well, it doesn't mean we'll find something suspicious. The day is long, and she might have done what she wanted earlier. Or she might not have even planned to do anything suspicious today. But we should follow her and find out," Emma said.

Curious, they both followed Penelope at a distance. They followed her down Napoleon Ave for a few minute, and then she appeared to have answered a phone call. They moved closer and hid so they could hear the conversations clearly.

"Yes? You can rest assured I'll get personal effects from them when I go to the Coven. I'll let you know." Penelope said so and hung up.

"Did you hear that?" Emma asked Evelyn, hiding behind a bush in a flowerbed.

"Yes, I heard. Though I suspected her, I can't believe she's really betraying us and stabbing us in the back like this," Evelyn said. "She was the one who took our personal objects and energetically connected us to Jonas' Coven."

"We have to tell everyone," Emma said.

The two went on foot, returning to the parking lot. Arriving at Emma's car, she invited Evelyn to come home with her. It was just the two of them in the car as they went home, disappointed and slightly angered by what they had just seen.

When they arrived at the house, Emma immediately started talking to Cedric. She couldn't wait to share what they'd just seen with him.

"Love, where are you?" Emma asked, looking for him past the living room.

"My God!" Emma screamed when she saw Cedric passed out on the floor.
"Come help me, Evelyn.". She called out, her plea for assistance underscored by a palpable sense of dread.

Evelyn by Emma's side, her presence a reassuring anchor amidst the chaos that had unfolded. Together, they cradled Cedric, their hands reaching out to him in a gesture of support and concern. Slowly, the veil of unconsciousness lifted, and Cedric began to stir, his eyes fluttering open.

"Are you okay, dear?" Emma asked, "What happened?". She inquired, the gravity of the situation demanding answers.

Evelyn's intuitive abilities came into play as she placed her hands on Cedric, channeling healing energy. "It was an energy attack," Evelyn intuited, her words resonating with a blend of knowledge and conviction.

Closing her eyes, Evelyn sought to pierce the veil that obscured the truth, her mind reaching out in search of the events that had led to Cedric's collapse. But the void that greeted her was an unsettling gray, a barrier that thwarted her attempts to glean insights.

"Something is trying to stop me from seeing, interfering with my visions," she confessed, her frustration palpable as she shared her struggle to make sense of the situation. "I see figures, dark spirits," she added, the gravity of her vision casting a shadow over the room.

Cedric, gathering his strength and resolve, rose to his feet, his determination undeterred by the sinister forces that had sought to weaken him.

"Baron Samedi, great master, protect us," he invoked, his words carrying a resonance of power and reverence.

"We have to counter-attack. Because in our fear, others see opportunities," Cedric declared, his voice a rallying call to action. "Let's get everyone together. We will operate with intelligence and silence," he instructed, his leadership emerging as a guiding light amidst the encroaching darkness.

Emma's words added another layer to the unfolding turmoil.
"Ok. But we discovered that Penelope had been working against us this whole time. Turns out you were right.
We followed her," she revealed, the revelation punctuating the room with a jolt of betrayal and realization.

"That bitch!" Cedric's exclamation reverberated, his anger a testament to the depth of the betrayal that had unfurled within their midst.

"May the devil cut off our enemies' feet so we can recognize them by their limps," Evelyn roared.

In the heart of their home, a battle raged—one that transcended the boundaries of the physical world and delved deep into the realms of the spiritual.
With Cedric, Emma, and Evelyn at the center of this storm, the stage was set for a confrontation that would test their bonds, challenge their beliefs, and unearth the secrets that lay shrouded in the mist of mystery and suspense.

Later, Penelope's entrance into the temple was met with a sea of disapproving glares, the accusing gazes of the coven members like daggers aimed at her conscience. She found herself standing at the epicenter of a storm, facing the wrath of those she had betrayed.

"So, traitor, you can still come here?" Emma's voice sliced through the air, each word a whip of accusation that reverberated with the weight of the revelations that had come to light.

"Traitor? Me? Why?" She asked, trying to sound and look innocent, not knowing she'd been caught red-handed.

Cedric's gaze bore into her, and his voice had a low, simmering undertone of disappointment and anger. "'Yes, we know everything you are doing," he began, his words ringing like a sentence pronounced by a judge. "And we know you're seeing Jonas behind our backs and that you are working against us.".

A brief pause hung in the air, a suspended moment in which Penelope's attempt to concoct a defense faltered. "But..." she began, only to be cut off by the resolute voice of Evelyn.

"It's no use saying anything, Emma, and I saw you get into his car," Evelyn interjected, her tone a mixture of scorn and reproach, her words like a gavel that had come down on Penelope's credibility.

The truth hung heavy in the air, a palpable admission that had Penelope grappling for words. She clung to half-truths and excuses, her voice straining as she tried to maintain the illusion of innocence. "He was blackmailing me and..."

Her voice trailed off, the weakness of her explanation reflecting the extent of her desperation.

"Don't bullshit," Leonard said.

Penelope burst into tears. She began to confess, "I already knew Jonas for a long time, and I had a great crush on him, even though he was with Isabella. We had an affair and sometimes..."

Cedric's voice was a blend of rage and heartbreak as he addressed her.
"You betrayed us! People died! You certainly provided Jonas with our personal items."

With crocodile tears, Penelope pleaded for forgiveness, her voice laced with desperation and remorse. "Forgive me," she implored, her words a desperate plea in the face of the devastation she had wrought.

Amidst the chaos of Penelope's confession and the coven's response, a new presence began to make itself known. Evelyn's senses tingled with an incoming energy, an ominous awareness that unfurled like tendrils of shadow.

"I feel someone coming here," she murmured amidst the turmoil, her words tinged with a sense of foreboding. "I sense a presence," she continued, her voice quivering as she unraveled the truth.
"It's... It's Jonas and the others, from the Coven Nightshadow Dew," She revealed, her words an announcement that heralded the arrival of another storm on the horizon.

Just then, there was a loud knock on the door. Cedric quickly went to check on who it was.

Cedric's incredulous voice laced with bitterness echoed through the room: "Yes, they are! What do you idiots want here?" His words were laden with simmering anger, an embodiment of the conflict that had divided them.

"Just talk." Jonas's words were a plea that veiled a hidden undercurrent of urgency. His demeanor seemed to have shifted from arrogance to something more complex, a subtle admission that the situation had escalated beyond his control.

But Emma's voice carried a storm of its own, her words punctuating the charged atmosphere with a sense of betrayal and accusation.

"Your traitorous friend, Penelope, is here," she called out, her voice carrying a weight of scorn and disappointment.

Jonas's gaze shifted to Penelope, who seemed to shrink under the weight of the collective condemnation. His words were cryptic, a maze of manipulation that spoke of hidden agendas and calculated maneuvers.

"Each person is a puzzle of needs," he stated, his tone a mix of condescension and arrogance. "You will have to intuit what needs they feel and become the essential piece, and that way they will be under your control".

"When the mind is blind, the eyes are meaningless," Evelyn mused, her words an enigmatic commentary on the complex web of manipulation that seemed to ensnare those present.

Amidst the maelstrom of emotions and confessions, Emma's presence suddenly shifted, her demeanor changing like the flip of a coin. The entity she had been channeling overtook her once more, her body a vessel for a voice that emanated from beyond the realm of the living. "Get ready, there will be war," the voice of the entity declared, its tone like the tolling of a distant bell, foretelling an impending storm.

Evelyn and Leonard acted with swiftness and determination, rushing to hold Emma's form as the entity's grip tightened.

The room was thick with the tension of the unknown, and the coven members held a delicate balance between apprehension and resolve.

Cedric's frustration was palpable, his voice echoing through the room as he grappled with the maelstrom of emotions and confusion that surged within him.

"But who is this voice? Identify yourself," he demanded, his words a manifestation of his yearning for clarity amidst the chaos that had enveloped their world.

In the core of the temple, secrets and mysteries intermingled, and the shadows cast by both external and internal conflicts seemed to stretch and contort, creating a tableau of uncertainty that painted the future with hues of both danger and opportunity.

(continue)

Chapter 5

"I am Anima Sola.". A shiver seemed to ripple through the room.

"Hmm... I know this entity; I've heard of it." Evelyn's words carried a mixture of awe and caution, her voice resonating with the weight of her spiritual wisdom.

"Now I have to go; powerful entities are on their way," said the spirit, leaving. The spirit's departure was as abrupt as its arrival, leaving a vacuum of silence in its wake.

Jonas, who had been a pillar of arrogance and confidence, suddenly found himself faltering, his legs trembling under the weight of an invisible force. "What's up? What's happening to me?" His voice trembled with a vulnerability that was alien to his usual demeanor.

Cedric's explanation brought a semblance of understanding to the unfolding situation. "It must be because we put magic powders and graveyard dirt on the street, where your footprints passed. It's foot track magic." Cedric's voice carried a mix of grim realization and resolution.

But the room was soon filled with a disconcerting symphony as rumblings akin to distant thunder rolled through the air. The lights flickered and danced erratically, casting shifting shadows that added to the surreal ambiance. The very atmosphere seemed to reverberate with an otherworldly energy, as if astral wolves were howling in the unseen realms.

With different shapes and figures, various entities emerged. A large serpent; it looked like Damballa. Various Eshús also appeared. Even the Santa Muerte of Latin occultism, the Baron Samedi of Vodoo.

"Dios mio, la huesuda! La dama Poderosa!" Exclaimed Isabella in Spanish. She'd also come with Jonas and stayed silently behind him.

The echoes of the spirits' presence reverberated in the air, their voices echoing as one. "I'm Santa Muerte. We are egregores that you have been energizing over the decades and in rituals. We fed on your energies, but we needed more, and fueling a war between the two Covens was ideal." The words, spoken in unison yet carrying unique undertones, bore the weight of truth and manipulation.

As the room pulsated with the presence of these formidable entities, the coven members stood in a state of shock and disbelief. The revelations unfolded before them like an intricate tapestry woven with threads of manipulation and power.
The words of Santa Muerte reverberated in the air, delivering the damning truth that their Covens had been pawns in a larger cosmic game.

"You started hating each other and doing more witchcraft against each other, and the energy vortex increased," she continued.

Baron Samedi, exuding an air of regal authority, continued the narrative. "But we are rival entities to each other, and now a spiritual battle will take place, choose your sides," his voice held an undercurrent of challenge, a stark reminder of the opposing forces that had manipulated them for their own purposes.

But then the scene shifted before their eyes. Damballa, the astral serpent, began to coil and move with graceful fluidity, enveloping Santa Muerte in its embrace. The Eshús, spirits of cunning and crossroads, manifested rays of astral fire that shot forth with blazing intensity, illuminating the room with an otherworldly glow.

Meanwhile, Santa Muerte, with his scythe, cuts the Damballa serpent into pieces astrally. Everything unfolded as if they were holographic projections in the air, and the attacks were in energetic form.

Everyone from both Covens looked on in horror.

"My God!" Evelyn exclaimed. Her words were laden with a mix of awe and fear, mirroring the sentiments of everyone present.

"Can we do something?" Asked Emma. Her eyes darted between the interplay of forces. The desperation in her voice was palpable, and the realization that they were spectators to an otherworldly clash left them feeling powerless.

The entities, their energies intertwining in a dance of primal power, turned their attention toward the coven members, addressing them once more.

"You humans never had power over us; we just pretended to be complicit during the rituals, but we followed our own agenda."

Cedric, his mind racing to find a solution, broke the tense silence.

"We must evoke an entity more powerful than all these! That's the only way." His eyes searched for a way to break the deadlock that had enveloped them all.

As the coven members embraced the decision to evoke Lucifer, a sense of unity prevailed, momentarily setting aside their differences. Even Jonas and Isabella, despite their initial skepticism, recognized the urgency of the situation and joined the circle of invocation.
The need for a powerful force to counter the malevolent entities had united them in a common goal.

"Yes, let's evoke Lucifer, the great prince of this world, the mighty archangel." Evelyn's voice cut through the charged atmosphere.

Her words resonated with determination, underscoring the gravity of their collective intent.
The urgency of their circumstances demanded that they set aside formalities and proceed swiftly.

The group quickly gathered their energies and focused their intentions, adapting their ritual to the exigent moment. The sacred space seemed to hum with anticipation, as if the very air was charged with their combined energy.

"O great Lucifer, the morning star. Lucifer in Excelsis. Glorious Be. We work in the shadows to make light." The words rolled off their tongues in unison, reverberating through the room. The power of their collective voice held a commanding quality, invoking the presence of the one they sought.

Everyone repeated in unison: "Lucifer in Excelsis."

"Lucifer, come and light this world of darkness and suffering. Mighty Lucifer comes to our calling." Cedric's voice rang out with authority, his energy intertwining with the others'.

And then, in a breathtaking moment, a brilliant flash of light burst forth, bathing the room in radiant luminescence. It was as if a celestial sun had momentarily descended, casting aside the shadows that had lingered.

The other entities dematerialized as they felt a vibration greater than theirs. The power of Lucifer's presence seemed to disperse them like mist before a strong wind.

With the energies shifting, the voice of Lucifer resonated within the minds of the coven members.

"Very well, they respected my spiritual authority and left; I put an order in the house. Now, in reciprocity, I hope that you worship only me. As you should all have done from the beginning."

His words were imbued with regal authority, a reminder of the symbiotic relationship they had entered into.

"Of course, master," they all said.

"Channel your energy to me alone; I can provide wisdom, spiritual protection, and enlightenment." Lucifer's voice echoed within their consciousness, his promises resonating with an alluring power.

"May the strong be blessed and the weak victims of their own weaknesses!"

Lucifer's proclamation reverberated, a chilling reminder of the duality inherent in his dominion. The entity that had answered their call demanded their loyalty and devotion, promising to guide them through the darkness while also embodying the harsh realities of power and hierarchy.

"I am Lucifer, Enki, Heylel; I am in everything, and everything is in Me; I am the true god of this world, divine and incorruptible essence... I make matter and movement the mirror of my conscience," he said.

They began to hear police sirens. Lucifer immediately became invisible and inconspicuous. Soon after, Agent Curtis and two others enter.

"What was that noise? Is there some fighting going on here?" Asked agent Curtis.

When no one responded, the agent went on, "Mr. Jonas, come with us. We now know that he had the braking system sabotaged in the vehicle that John and Wilbour drove."

"But I didn't do anything," Jonas said.

"It's no use denying it. We interrogated a guy named Paul Weaver for several hours; we squeezed him tight, and he confessed who hired him."

"Babe, call our lawyer!" Jonas said to Isabella as they grabbed him. The agents handcuffed him and took him away.

"Cariño, no!..." Murmured Isabella without being able to do anything.

The aftermath of the confrontation had left its mark on everyone present, and Cedric's Coven knew they had to act swiftly to prevent further harm from coming to them. Isabella, the remaining member of Nightshadow Dew, was advised to leave before the situation escalated any further. She departed, casting a defiant glare back at them; her departure marked the end of a bitter chapter.

"Vete al carajo," she said, leaving.

After she left, Lucifer became visible again. His ethereal form exuded a sense of power and otherworldly authority, a stark reminder of the pact they had forged.

"To have my protection, work for me." Lucifer's voice resonated, commanding attention. His words were both an offer and an expectation, a reminder that the terms of their newfound alliance required reciprocity.

Evelyn, never one to shy away from asking the pertinent questions, voiced the thoughts that had been simmering in their minds.

"You want our souls, don't you?" Her words hung in the air, carrying the weight of suspicion.

Lucifer's laughter echoed, filling the room with an eerie resonance.

"Do you think you're going to heaven with the crap you've done throughout your lives?" He retorted. His words were a stark reminder that their moral choices and actions held consequences that reached beyond the earthly realm.

"The sky is an illusion, and it is a desert. In fact, millions of souls are always reincarnating, the cycle of Samsara does not stop," Lucifer elucidated, his voice a cryptic blend of truth and enigma.

Evelyn's brows furrowed in contemplation, the weight of Lucifer's words settling upon her. Before anyone could respond, Lucifer's instruction shifted the conversation toward the path that lay ahead.

"Recruit thousands of new souls and members to the Coven; expand and open new temples, recruit online, whatever is necessary,"

Lucifer's directive was clear. The very essence of their survival hinged on their ability to gather forces, strengthen their ranks, and extend their influence.

Cedric, standing at the center of the room, absorbed Lucifer's words with a sense of resolve. "If that is all there really has to be to have your protection, then we will do so," he affirmed, determination igniting within him.

The weight of the challenge was met with a fierce commitment to protect their coven and uphold their newfound alliance.

Lucifer's form flickered for a moment, a wry smile playing at the corners of his ethereal countenance.

"This is how Scientology started. Freemasonry also owes me reverence." His voice carried an air of intrigue, hinting at the intricate web of influence and power that transcended the earthly realm.

With his final words, Lucifer's presence began to dissolve, leaving the coven members to grapple with the implications of their choices.

As the echoes of his departure lingered, the room seemed charged with both anticipation and trepidation. Their path forward was marked by uncertainty, alliances forged in the shadows, and a destiny intertwined with the enigmatic forces that govern the occult realm.

Chapter 6

There would be war...

Emma kept muttering through the night in her feverish state as her eyes rolled in her head. Cedric stayed up all night, washing her body with cold water to keep her temperature down. He was frightened for her and, more importantly, for their future.

What will happen next? Who would die next? With the police holding Jonas, and the rival Coven seething with anger, and Emma having these strange spasms, he wondered what was next.

The storm had been pouring outside for hours, and the thunder echoed through the house every time a peal rumbled across the sky. The electricity had shut off long ago. It felt ominous, like the world was ending, and he knew he had to prepare.

The ancestral Covens are at war, and if he doesn't prepare his people, it might be catastrophic.

Cedric laid beside Emma, patting her and whispering gentle words to her to soothe whatever pain she was feeling. He loved her, and now he felt terribly incapacitated and impotent.

Cedric woke up to a sudden bang on the door of his home. He rushed to it to find Penelope. After banishment, he didn't think she'd dare to show her face again, but he could see the desperation in them, and aside from that, the streak of blood that poured from her nose made it alarming.

"He escaped!" she said crying. "Jonas escaped from jail."

"What?!" Cedric was wild. How could that be? How? Possibly he had help from allies inside the prison.

The enigmatic forces that had guided his actions were still at play, and Jonas was determined to navigate the labyrinthine world of occult politics and power on his own terms.

Cedric couldn't trust Penelope, but why would she like? What would she gain? And why wouldn't she tell him this sooner? Why not just get out and hide somewhere in the countryside, where no one would recognize her?

Cedric's frustration grew. Penelope had been manipulated too, a pawn in this larger game. He wanted to shake her, to demand answers, but he knew that wasn't the way to get the truth.

"We need to know everything. Who are these shadows? What do they want? And why did they help Jonas escape?"

Penelope's lips quivered, tears mixing with the rain on her cheeks. "They... They want chaos. They want the Covens to tear each other apart. They feed off the energy of the conflict, and they promised Jonas power in exchange for his loyalty."

Cedric's mind raced. The storm outside intensified, as though nature itself was reacting to the darkness that had been unleashed. He couldn't allow this chaos to consume them and destroy everything they had worked for.

Emma's voice cut through the turmoil, her presence surprising both Cedric and Penelope. "She's a Trojan horse."

"What do you mean?"

Emma's eyes held an intensity that Cedric had rarely seen.

"They used her to infiltrate our ranks, to gather information, and to sow discord. Penelope wasn't just an innocent victim; she was a pawn in their game."

Evelyn, who had seen such a vision, rushed into the scene, panting as she reached the door where Cedric stood over Penelope as she took.

ric's mind raced, connecting the dots. Penelope's sudden arance, her panic, the streak of blood. It all makes sense now.

She had been sent to deliver this message, to disrupt their unity, to plant seeds of doubt and fear.

Evelyn immediately recited some spells and bent over the dying Penelope.
For the first time, Cedric sees the conflicting emotions on Evelyn's face. She felt as impotent as he had been yesterday.

Evelyn could not help Penelope. Nobody could; this was the first sign of the raging battle. Penelope stopped moving, and her body slowly disintegrated into dust.

Evelyn looked up at Cedric with immense sorrow in her eyes. She felt tears run down her cheeks as she realized that a part of her might have felt something for Penelope all this while.

"We need to warn the others!" She said, toughening herself. She needed to prepare for battle just like anyone else. It was pointless to cry over Penelope at this point.
The only way to get justice is to win.

"Jonas has escaped. His Coven is planning..."

Immediately, Cedric swung into action, calling all his people to the old temple with the help of Evelyn.

The opposition was going to play dirty. They were going to lead the war into the lives of innocent people, and Cedric had to stop that first. The last thing he wanted was to have unnecessary deaths.

People would die for no reason, and that was the height of the sinister mind of the opposition. He needs to fight them fair and square, although he is unsure how to do that because he doesn't know how they will act.

Immediately, the entire Coven gathered at the old temple and started to chant incantations, calling on the devil to come to their aid. Althou this was not a battle they started, this would be a battle they would end.

"We need a sacrifice." Said Evelyn as she closed her eyes and began to focus.

"If we don't get Jonas and make him submit peacefully, everyone else will get hurt. He must live, or there will be consequences."

But this was beyond submission. Jonas had made his choice to fight an ancestral battle, and he would not stop till they all burned down. He has Isabella with him. She has the power and influence, and it's only a matter of time before hell opens.

"I will do it," Emma said, stepping into the middle of the circle they had created and starting to undress. To please the devil, you must be in your absolute form, and her absolute form was her nudity and soul.

Cedric charged at her, stopping her.

"What the hell are you doing?!" He stopped her, pulling her robe around her. "Are you crazy?"

"There is no other way." She smiled sadly. "I need to subject myself to him; let him take me so he can give you all redemption.

"You are insane!" he roared at her. "We are going to fight, and we are going to win. There is no chance in hell that I will give you up, never!"

Evelyn kept chanting, reciting the incantations along with the other members.

Cedric felt his chest squeeze with apprehension for such. He had lost too many members in a matter of days, and he was not ready to lose the love of his life as well.
He held on to Emma and hugged her tighter against his chest, afraid to let her leave his embrace.
This might be the end, and they might not survive it.

"Love, let's fight. Let's fight." But, Emma had seen how it would end.
He saw death waiting for them all if they did not surrender their lives.

a..." said Cedric softly and pleadingly, "we are going to survive

We have survived worse things, and we will survive this! You can't give your life to another just because you feel sorry for me."

But her eyes were closed, and she was slipping away from him.

"No!" He yelled and screamed until the voices of the witches and the demon came back to him.

"It won't work! It's not a sacrifice! Emmaaa!" he shouted in vain.

Her eyes opened as if trying to consume his sight for the last time. However, it was because she saw them coming. They had a large army, and they were coming for them.

Jonas had gotten a higher power, and he was drunk on it. She could see him transforming into a beast that would devour everything.

They were surrounded by dark energy. He had to get her far enough away from here; she knew that much.

Cedric tried his best to keep her close, even as his strength waned and she felt herself slipping away from him. She couldn't stay in this form, but she was willing to sacrifice herself for her Coven.
Even though she knows Cedric can fight this, he would surely die without her protection. She would die with him, and she wanted him to live.
He had to continue living his normal life, leading the "Hidden Hand" to the promised land.

"They are here." Evelyn could see it too.

The temple doors opened, and Jonas instantly led his army of witches and wizards into the battleground.

Cedric's Coven stopped chanting and prepared to attack. Cedric thought that if he spoke to Jonas one last time, they might reach a compromise, but Jonas was not in there anymore. It was as if he had been taken on by the worst kind of demon, using him mercilessly to create havoc and instability in the Coven.
It seemed to be their fate.

With great power came great chaos, and they will fight to the limit.

But there is something in between, and the witch and wizard are caught in a conflict between lesser good and greater evil. In this war of bad and evil, who will prevail, what will happen, and what shall become of the world?
The future is always changing, never staying in one place. And in this case, those who should have known better than to fall prey to the temptations of lust and passion have, and there is no turning back.

If there had been a time when they could have lived happily ever after, it has long since passed. Now their story has begun anew. The future was about to change forever if they did not stop it. If they did not save their world.

They were fighting hard with all they had. Some sacrifices were made, but others had to be sacrificed.

They all wanted to protect each other and live as long as they had any hope of survival.

They had to finish this once and for all in order to bring peace to the world. That was the only thing stopping this madness from tearing them apart.

But, as usual, life has no sense of fairness, for even in this darkest moment, there was light at the end of the tunnel for them as they all stood together, united, fighting.

They could hear the sound of horns blowing in the distance, indicating that the battle was not yet finished. Jonas and his followers had arrived.

They attacked as soon as they arrived, and the fight turned ugly. small group of men, led by Jonas himself, had found an opening in enemy lines.

s and his army were unstoppable, and the witches and wizards out cries as they fought.

The witches and wizards were not fighters; they were trained in defense, not attacking or defending themselves as the warriors did. Many died from wounds and injuries caused by the demons, and Cedric was able to take them down quickly.

However, there were other forces that had joined Jonas.
Men wearing black leather armor, carrying weapons that glinted with deadly power. They outnumbered the witches and wizards many times. These enemies were diferente; they were more like demons themselves, and not a single one of them could be defeated.

Somehow, the two sides were still in a stalemate, neither gaining any victory. No matter which side you look at it from, they both needed each other. Cedric was getting tired and knew there was no way to stand his ground against these forces.
They were fighting to kill each other.

Cedric tried to call Jonas to see the reasons, but the reason was a fool's plan.

Evelyn recited a spell, sending half of Jonas's Coven against the brutal walls of the temple.

She was mad with rage.

Isabella, on the other hand, faced Emma. Emma was trying to get in touch with higher forces. She went on her knees, stripping off her blouse as she chanted several spells.

Isabella interrupted her with a blow to the head, forcing Emma to drop her blouse and lie down as she struggled and begged in vain, begging for mercy and salvation from the higher powers.

Evelyn stood alone at a point near where Isabella was standing.
Her eyes had darkened, and she could feel the power that had been locked within the stone and was now released through her body and towards the heavens.

Her hands were glowing green, and as the energies reached the s there was a loud thundering noise, like a thunderous roar, spread throughout the air.

When everything settled again, Evelyn lifted her face and watched as the dark figures of the demons retreated. As if they had never even existed. It was like they had simply melted away, and when she looked to the other side, the Coven had already taken control of the situation.

The remaining demons scattered, retreating to the edges of the field until they completely disappeared into thin air.

hey were in disbelief and astonished to see this.

s point, there was a strident sound like thunder. The atmosphere ed to thicken, making it difficult to breathe. Panic flickered in their fading awareness as their bodies succumbed to an overwhelming force. They fell to the ground and lost consciousness.

Santa Muerte had eradicated all oxygen in the area.

Without wanting to go into too many technical details, Santa Muerte manages to manipulate the astral aether, the astral energy, raising the temperature and breaking the oxygen molecules. It also altered and relieved the atmospheric pressure in that room; the air molecules dispersed, making the breathable oxygen more rarefied.

The outside air pressure became lower than the pressure inside their lungs, and with difficulty breathing, they collapsed.

After what felt like an eternity of unconsciousness, Evelyne's senses gradually awakened. She blinked, her surroundings coming into focus. But the silence that enveloped her was eerie and unsettling. It was as if the world had been muted, leaving her in a realm of profound stillness.

As her gaze wandered, she noticed a strange phenomenon. A luminous mist hung in the air, shifting between shades of golden and purple, casting an ethereal glow over everything.

Evelyne felt a shiver run down her spine as she realized that she was no longer in the familiar realm she had known. This was something different, something beyond the boundaries of her understanding.

It was a lower astral plane; the astral plane has several layers, and she was in the lowest and densest. Amidst the nebulous atmosphere, figures began to materialize.

They took shape, and gradually Evelyne recognized them. Isabella, Jonas, and the other members of the Coven stood before her, their features set in an otherworldly semblance. But there was an undercurrent of darkness —an aura that hinted at something far more powerful than the magic they had wielded before.

As the weight of the entities' presence settled upon the group, an otherworldly hush descended, their energy and power palpable.

Evelyne could feel their energy and power radiating like an electric charge in the air. It was as though the very fabric of reality had bent to accommodate their presence.

Then a procession of entities emerged from the shifting mist.

Lucifer, Santa Muerte, Nergal, Paymon, Bechard, and other entities decreed:

"From now on,"- their voices echoed in a chorus that reverberated through the very fabric of reality; "you will integrate our phalanges and work for us in the astral realm."

"Recruit more souls to work in this sector, mediumically inspire the written works of some witches on Earth (via telepathy), maintain the energies of rituals and offerings left in temples and crossroads, and you will do all the tasks we say."

"Your war was keeping two energetic currents between the Covens apart, dissipating energies now, and preventing new souls from joining witchcraft, which was counterproductive."

"You are now dark souls".

"Black souls?" The question quivered on their lips, their eyes wide with trepidation.

The response came swiftly and authoritatively:

"Yes, there are stars that, when they extinguish their gravitational ˀnter, colapse and become black holes; certain people when they ˀ their light, become a dark soul."

ˀn's voice, trembling with a mixture of confusion and a yearning ˀerstanding, pierced the air.

ˀe were alive," she ventured, her words carrying a poignant f realization.

The entities regarded her with a depth of wisdom that stretched across eons.

"Was that life? Sometimes the body and mind are a prison." Said Lucifer.

"Now you will be agents of our phalanxes. Keep calm. Behind every shadow, there is always a light.". They intoned, their words resonating as a mantra of hope.

The cosmic beings began to fade, their presence gradually receding like the shimmer of distant stars, leaving all of them in a state of profound reflection.

Their journey had taken an unforeseen turn, thrusting them into a realm where darkness and light converged.

The landscape around them bore a haunting resemblance to the corridors of dreams, where reality shifted and fractured like a broken mirror.

The presence of the entities that had thrust them into this enigmatic realm was both a source of guidance and a constant reminder of the irrevocable transformation they had undergone.

 As they embraced this new path, they found solace in the knowledge that even in the embrace of the unknown, there would always be the guiding presence of the entities and the promise of a hidden light waiting to be unveiled.

The End

Aleena Bot is a pseudonym.

The 39-year-old author has been a researcher in the paranormal, occultism, spiritualism and parapsychology for several years, but these topics are controversial and sometimes raise criticism from society.

Thus, the author assumed the pseudonym.

Her tales combine science fiction with the paranormal, much of the information being based on the author's own spiritual channelings or real situations of occult phenomena.

Your review, will be appreciated.

Other books by Aleena:

"Digital Dreams".

"From Bullying to Possession"

"Tainted Fantasies"

"Hyperdimensional Interference" (soon)